Schoolies™

The School Fair

Based on the characters created by
Ellen Crimi-Trent

priddy books

It was time for the School Fair.

Daisy Elephant Fish Globe House Ice cream

Everyone hoped to raise money
for a new playground slide.

All the Schoolies wanted to help make the fair a big success...

...but Spencer wanted the new slide more than anyone.

He decided he would work hard for it!

First, Spencer tried
to make the posters.

Glue and paint went everywhere!

Then Spencer
tried to set up the
lemonade stand...

Spencer looked at the spilled
paint and sticky food. He sighed.

Spencer got a clipboard and a pencil.
He wrote a list of jobs and asked for helpers.

Soon all the Schoolies were
busy doing what they did best.

C.J. Crawley stepped up to paint the posters.

Zippy hung up the bunting.

Hayden Hoot and Chip made
a maths game with prizes.

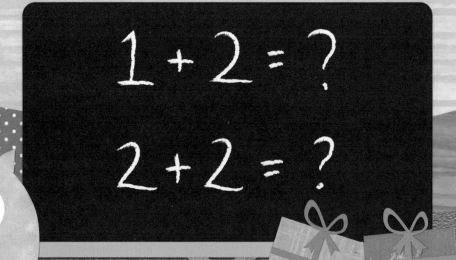

Spencer looked around
at all the busy Schoolies.
Everyone had something
important to do except him.

Cakes for

It was time for the fair to open! All the families came and had a great time.